TALKING TO THE DEVIL

Talking to the Devil
Copyright © 2022 by Clarence Causby

Published in the United States of America
ISBN   Paperback: 978-1-959165-51-4
ISBN   eBook: 978-1-959165-52-1

All rights reserved. No part of this publication may be reproduced, stored in a retrieval system or transmitted in any way by any means, electronic, mechanical, photocopy, recording or otherwise without the prior permission of the author except as provided by USA copyright law.

The opinions expressed by the author are not necessarily those of ReadersMagnet, LLC.

ReadersMagnet, LLC
10620 Treena Street, Suite 230 | San Diego, California, 92131 USA
1.619. 354. 2643 | www.readersmagnet.com

Book design copyright © 2022 by ReadersMagnet, LLC. All rights reserved.

Cover design by Kent Gabutin
Interior design by Daniel Lopez

TALKING TO THE DEVIL

CLARENCE CAUSBY

ReadersMagnet, LLC

CHAPTER 1

God was looking down from Heaven.

"What are you looking at Father?" said Jesus.

"I'm looking at Gary Winscombe. He's about to ask me if he can speak to Lucifer because he wants to ask him questions about why there is so much pain and sickness and everything in the world. Lucifer, Gary Winscombe wants to have a talk with you."

"Why does he want to speak to me?" asked Lucifer.

"He wants to have a conversation on why you're bringing the world so much pain and misery."

Lucifer started laughing, "All the pain I'm causing?" Lucifer couldn't stop laughing. "So what's supposed to happen now? You wouldn't have called me if it was just about him wanting to talk to me," said Lucifer.

"I want you to talk to him and answer his questions truthfully, but you are not allowed to kill him," said God. "He's about to ask me to speak with you, so go and talk to him." God added.

"This reminds me of the time when you wanted me to try Job. Fine, but is this a one-sided question, or do I get to ask him some things as well?" asked Lucifer.

"You can ask him questions," said God.

"God, I'm sick of Lucifer and everything he's doing to people. I want to talk to him and give him a piece of my mind about what he's doing," said Gary.

Gary was a man with a gray hoodie and black sweatpants. He was 225 pounds. He lived in New York City. He had black hair, a buzz cut and a goatee. He was light-skinned.

"Speak to him," said God.

"I really want to talk to him," said Gary.

"Now speak to him," God replied.

"Do I yell or talk to him like I'm talking to you now?" asked Gary.

He heard someone singing. Gary was on the street at nighttime and there were cars passing by, blowing their horns. He was standing at the edge of an alleyway. He saw a tall, slender man with blonde hair, hands in his pockets, singing.

The man walked up to Gary. "You called?"

Gary looked at the man with a confused look on his face. "I didn't call you, Sir, you have the wrong guy." Gary turned back around and said to himself, "God how do I go about talking to him?"

The man raised an eyebrow. "What do you want?" he asked. "You called, and now I'm here."

Gary turned around, annoyed at the man. "Sir, if you don't mind, I'm not talking to you and I didn't call for you. I don't know if you're homeless, I mean you don't look homeless. Just go on about your way, you're annoying me."

The man smirked. Gary turned around again. "God, can I please talk to him?" asked Gary.

"Talk to him," God replied.

"I said I'm here, now what do you want?" the man said.

Gary turned around. "If you don't leave me alone I will hit you. Now piss off you bum."

The man became angry. "You asked God to speak to me and I'm here. You asked God to speak to Lucifer. I'm Lucifer." Lucifer said in a demonic voice.

"You're not Lucifer," said Gary. "You don't have any wings and..."

Before Gary could get another word out, Lucifer said, "How stupid are you? You want the horns, the tail, the wings and all of that right? And even that insulting image of me being red with a pitchfork? Do you mortals really think for one second you would be able to stand to see my true form? You would be terrified and wouldn't be able to move," said Lucifer.

"That is true," replied Gary.

"So listen, you want to talk and we can talk. God has also forbidden me to kill you. Almost like it was with Job," said Lucifer.

"Oh wow I'm so excited, I'm just like Job."

Lucifer busted out in laughter. "You dare compare yourself with Job?" Lucifer laughed hysterically. "You're nowhere close to being like Job and you never will be. The majority of you mortals will never even reach an inch of where Job was." Lucifer continued to laugh.

Gary was angry, so he punched Lucifer. Gary's fist hit Lucifer's chest.

Lucifer immediately stopped laughing and said in a demonic voice, "You don't get who you're dealing with, do you? That's okay, because you're about to really learn who I am."

Lucifer disappeared. Gary looked around and saw Lucifer appear next to a car. Gary saw Lucifer talk to the guy in the car. The guy sped towards Gary and crashed an inch from him on his left. Gary was shocked and scared before he tried to move to the right. The car crashed and a sofa landed right next to him on his right. Gary was terrified and dropped to the ground with his back up against a small fence.

"Hey buddy!" cried a voice. Gary looked up terrified and saw a man yelling. "Sorry about that. I was trying to find a faster way of getting this sofa to the garbage. Are you good?" asked a guy from the roof of his building.

Gary was shaking. In a trembling voice he repied, "I'm okay."

Lucifer appeared, squatting down in front of him.

"You said you're not allowed to kill me, but you almost did," Gary said.

"You being killed and *almost* being killed are two different things. Understand this, and understand it well: "if you think trying to throw a punch at me will save you from me, you're sadly mistaken. Are you ready to talk now, or will I have to keep doing this?"

Gary couldn't say a word. He turned to the side and couldn't look at Lucifer.

"Don't get scared now, after all, weren't you the one trying to be so tough so you hit me with your fist?" said Lucifer. Lucifer picked up Gary. "Why are you not talking now, huh? You're not so tough, huh? You weren't going to hit me when you didn't know me, then when you found out it was me, you hit me and now you're not saying a word. I would love to kill you now. I really would because you're wasting my time. Here I am with you wanting to talk, then you try to act out in violence." Lucifer's voice changed to his demonic tone. "Look at me." Gary was too afraid to look. "I said, look at me!" Lucifer yelled. Gary turned and looked and started to cry. Lucifer dropped Gary on the ground. "Don't get scared now." Lucifer let out a sigh, "You mortals are so annoying. I don't know why any of you are still living. I couldn't be God because I would have killed all of you," said Lucifer. "God can you give him peace so we can talk and get this over with?"

Peace came upon Gary. "Now get up," said Lucifer.

The cops came. "Sir, are you okay? What happened?" Gary told them about the car coming close to him and almost hitting him.

The guy in the car was crying. "I'm so sorry," he said. "I was so angry. I wanted to end my life. I didn't even see you. I was hoping the crash would kill me." The guy in the car kept sobbing uncontrollably. "I'm so sorry. Please, please, kill me," said the guy to the cops.

"Sir, we are not going to kill you. We just want to get you some help, buddy. Come on. We're going to put some handcuffs on you, okay? We're going to try and get you some help," one of the officers said.

"Are you sure you're okay, Sir?" said the other officer.

"Yes, I'm fine, thank you," Gary replied. Gary got up.

The guy from the top of the building came and told the officers what happened about the sofa. The cops looked at Gary in disbelief. "Sir, let the paramedics take a look at you. You seem to be one lucky person to not die or get horribly injured by this car or the sofa. Why do you even have a sofa up there anyways, and what is your name?" The cops asked the guy who had dropped the sofa.

"Well, it's so nice up here on the roof, we wanted to be able to sit out here in the evenings. My name is Paul."

"Okay Paul, be more careful next time. It looks like you will have to get a new sofa," said the cop.

"I definitely will, sorry about all of this, and thank you."

The cops took the guy from the car and put him in the police car and were on their way to take him to the hospital.

"Let's go to your apartment," said Lucifer.

"Why?" asked Gary.

"Because you're the only one who can see me, and if you're seen talking to yourself, you'll be right on your way to the mental hospital."

"I hadn't thought about that," said Gary.

"You mortals never seem to think a whole lot do you?" asked Lucifer.

"You're awfully rude," said Gary.

"And you're awfully stupid," Lucifer replied. "You seem stressed, like you've had a hard day at work."

"I have. It's annoying."

"You look like you could even use a cigarette," said Lucifer.

"I don't smoke, but have always wanted to try it," replied Gary.

"So go and buy a pack and give it a try," said Lucifer.

"No, I'm not going to smoke at all," replied Gary.

"But you want to try it right? You've heard people talk about how relaxing it is. You should give it a try and just see. What could it hurt?" said Lucifer

"I don't know," said Gary, "then again, like you said, what could it hurt?" Gary and Lucifer were passing a store. Gary stopped and went into the store and bought some cigarettes. After coming out of the store, Gary and Lucifer went to Gary's apartment. Gary opened the door and sat down in his recliner. He let out a sigh of relief. He looked across from him as Lucifer sat straight in his chair, ,right leg crossed over his left leg, hands folded. He could see Lucifer's shadow, it had huge wings.

"You look thirsty. Why don't you go and make yourself a drink and get something to eat so you can fully relax?" said Lucifer.

"I think I will get some water," replied Gary.

"You know, maybe you don't want any water. You had a rough day today. Your boss was being a pain and kept getting on your case. You need a strong drink," said Lucifer.

"No, I won't. I haven't had a drink in six months and I'm proud of myself." Gary said.

"Yeah, but why do you still have the vodka and the gin bottles in your cabinets now? Why not throw them out? Come on, what is the big deal? You earned yourself a drink or two. You know you want some. It's not going to kill you, it's only you and me here. Who's going to know? I know you told a few people that you were sober, but if they're not here, how will they ever find out?" said Lucifer.

"You're right," replied Gary. Gary got up, got a glass, poured himself some whiskey and warmed up some food. He came back and sat down.

"So we can get started with me talking to you and asking you questions." Gary finished his glass of whiskey. He was eating leftover chicken and rice.

"You should pour yourself another glass," said Lucifer.

"I think I've had enough, one glass was good," said Gary.

"I bet it must have tasted so delicious and went down smooth, didn't it?" asked Lucifer.

"It sure did," replied Gary.

"Well, drink another one and then we can get started. I want to make sure you're good and ready to go with what you want to talk about."

Gary poured another glass. He took a sip. "That tasted so good to me," said Gary. He looked up and saw Lucifer smiling. To Gary, Lucifer's smile was unnerving. "What are you smiling at?" asked Gary.

"Oh nothing, just want to make sure you're enjoying your dinner and drink." Lucifer replied.

"I want to ask you some questions," said Gary.

"What questions would you like to ask me?" asked Lucifer.

"I want to know why you make people kill people? Why do you cause people to commit suicide? And why do you have people that have no money come to church? Also, why do you make people leave the church for good? I have other questions as well."

Lucifer raised an eyebrow. The smile he had disappeared. While in the chair, he uncrossed his legs and leaned forward. "So let me get this straight, you want to ask me those questions, am I right?"

"Yes," said Gary, "because I have a lot to get off my chest with you."

"Okay, so let me ask you some questions then, too, because I have a ton of questions and things I want to get off of my chest with you stupid Christians," said Lucifer coldly.

Gary was taken aback by that, and was shocked. "We're not stupid," replied Gary, "and how do I even know you'll be telling the truth?"

"Because God told me to tell you the truth and to be as truthful as I can be." said Lucifer.

"God, did you tell Lucifer to tell me the truth?"

"Yes," replied God.

"You see, I told you," Lucifer replied.

"So the first question I want to ask is..." Before Gary could get another word out, he was interrupted.

"You wanted to know why I make people do all these horrible things right? Which is pretty much the general question right? Why do I, Lucifer, make these people do anything right?"

"Yes," said Gary.

"Okay, I'm going to answer your question with a question."

Gary was confused. "What do you mean by that?"

"What makes you and all these other dumb Christians think I make people do anything?" asked Lucifer.

"You do. You made Eve eat the apple, you make people kill others, you make people commit suicide," replied Gary.

Lucifer looked at Gary. "Well, let's start with Eve. You said I made Eve eat the apple right?"

"You did," said Gary.

"Where in the bible did it say I made her eat the apple?" replied Lucifer. "Does it say in the bible that I transformed into this form and forced her to eat an apple? Did it say I told her if she didn't eat the apple, that I would kill her and Adam? Does it say that as the snake, I told her if she doesn't eat of the apple, that I would bite her and inject venom into her and that she would die? Does it say anywhere in any bible that I held her and forced her to eat the apple?" asked Lucifer.

"Well, no, but you made her do it, though," said Gary.

"Get your bible. Go ahead and get it."

Gary did as he was told and sat back down.

"Turn to Genesis chapter three. What does it say? Read it," said Lucifer.

" Now the serpent was subtler than any beast of the field which the Lord God had made. And he said unto the woman, 'Yea, hath God said, Ye shall not eat of every tree of the garden?'

And the woman said unto the serpent, 'we may eat of the fruit of the trees of the garden:

But of the fruit of the tree which is in the midst of the garden, God hath said, Ye shall not eat of it, neither shall ye touch it, lest ye die.'

And the serpent said unto the woman,' Ye shall not surely die:

For God doth know that in the day ye eat thereof, then your eyes shall be opened, and ye shall be as gods, knowing good and evil.'

And when the woman saw that the tree was good for food, and that it was pleasant to the eyes, and a tree to be desired to make one wise, she took of the fruit thereof, and did eat, and gave also unto her husband with her; and he did eat."

"Does it say that the serpent made her do it?" asked Lucifer.

"No," Gary replied.

"What does it say I did?" asked Lucifer.

"The bible says you spoke to Eve," Gary replied.

"Stop right there," said Lucifer. "So that's all it says?" he asked.

"Yes," said Gary.

"Well, I don't want you to have any doubts. Check on that phone or computer of yours and look up different bibles and see if it says the same thing, or similar," said Lucifer.

Gary looked at different versions. "It pretty much says the same thing. One did say 'asked' and another said you spoke," said Gary.

"So let me get this straight, it says I just spoke to Eve. Did it say anything about me forcing her, or me threatening her, or turning into this form and physically grabbing her and forcing her to eat?" asked Lucifer.

"Well, no… but…"

"There are no buts at all. You say you believe in the bible, or do you think the bible is lying? Have you ever heard preachers say,'Oh the devil is a strategist or a tactician?" asked Lucifer.

"Yes, I've heard a few preachers say that." replied Gary.

"So if I'm a strategist, why would I need to get my hands dirty? As you read in the bible, I merely spoke. I was giving suggestions and implying things. I didn't force her to do anything. So let me ask you a question," Lucifer said, "do you believe that guns kill?"

"Of course they do," replied Gary.

"Wrong," said Lucifer.

"What do you mean 'wrong'?," replied Gary harshly.

"Watch your mouth," said Lucifer. "The only way a gun can kill a person is if you take a gun itself and beat someone to death with it. Then, if they die, then yes a gun killed a person. But a gun doesn't kill anyone. If fired, the bullet is the thing that kills the person. Here look at this," said Lucifer. Lucifer put out his hand, palm facing up. A bullet appeared in his hand. Lucifer handed the bullet to Gary. "Okay, so what is the bullet doing now?"

"Nothing," said Gary. "So now a bullet can't kill anybody in this state right?"

"You're right, it can't do anything without a gun."

A gun then appeared in Lucifer's hand. He placed the gun in Gary's hand. "With the gun and the bullet where they are now, can they kill anyone?"

"No, you have to put the bullet in the gun."

"Gary, in the current state of the gun and the bullet now, with the bullet laying in your hand alongside the gun in your hand, the bullet not loaded in the gun, can they kill people as they are now?"

"No," Gary said.

"Now put the bullet in the gun, don't even try to point it at me. Just put the bullet in the gun and lay the gun back down in your hand." Gary did as Lucifer asked.

"Can the bullet be fired now and kill someone, from that position?"

"No," Gary replied.

"Right," said Lucifer. "You need a person to pull the trigger." The gun disappeared from Gary's hand. "The gun and the bullets are tools to kill someone. I use your weaknesses; I use your insecurities. For example, the car that you thought was going to kill you, the driver wanted to end his life. All I told him was to drive into that wall, and with enough impact, he would die, and that the hardest part of the wall that would surely kill him was next to you. So that's what happened. If your weakness is women, I'll get a very attractive woman to walk past or even flirt with you or to say 'hi'."

If your weakness is food, while you're on a diet or fasting, I'll make sure commercials come on with nothing but food on, or I'll have someone cook something and make sure you are within distance of smelling the food. When I get involved with someone who wants to commit suicide, I bring up everything they hate about themselves or about life. I implant thoughts and I whisper, 'go ahead, you know the world would be better without you.' I make all the pressures and the sense of hopelessness increase and tell them it will never get better. I make them feel like they are drowning in a world of problems and make them feel like they will never come up for air. I don't physically kill anyone," said Lucifer.

"Now as far as me making someone kill other people, sometimes I do, because I get a little enjoyment out of it, especially when it involves church people, now that is truly enjoyable to me. Some people kill people because they want to. I do have my demons reside in a city. Why do you think some cities have a higher crime rate than others? I don't always have people or have demons telling people to kill others. Sometimes they do it on their own because of jealousy, because they want another person's spouse, or they don't like the fact that someone disagreed with them, or they see someone has something that they don't have. Or sometimes, it could be as simple as someone got on their nerves and made them so mad that they just want to lash out and kill them. Sometimes, when they're doing something wrong and they get called out or beaten up for it because of something they did to someone else's loved one or some business arrangement, they then feel like they've been disrespected and feel like the only way to get justice for themselves is to kill someone or kill the person that made them feel that way. So like I said, sometimes I do have a part in it and sometimes I don't," he explained

"About your other question, why do I make people come to church with no money, that's what you're asking right?"

"Yes," replied Gary.

"What is church to you? Why do you think people should come to church?" asked Lucifer.

"Church is a place where we come together to learn about God. Plus, they need to come and pay their tithes. If they don't then they don't need to even be at church. Even with offerings, other people give dollars. If offerings are all they give, then they have no right to be prayed for. If you know you are coming to church, then you should have everything in order."

"You should bring money and come dressed up all the time?"

"You shouldn't dress in any kind of way," said Gary.

"So you're telling me that you need money to go to church? You're also telling me that churches charge for prayers? Do churches have an entry fee now as well? I'll even give you a quarter of a point about the dressing, but I'll touch on that in a minute."

"No churches don't charge an entry fee, but the bible says, in Malachi 3:8, 'Will a man rob God? Yet ye have robbed me. But ye say, wherein have we robbed thee? In tithes and offerings,'" Said Gary.

"So let me get this straight," Lucifer said. "If a homeless person decides to come into church, you would turn him away?"

"No, we wouldn't turn him away, unless he stunk," replied Gary.

"Okay," said Lucifer. "So you want to turn homeless people away, those who have nowhere or any place to wash up, that is, of course they went into a restaurant to clean themselves up. But yet, what if they don't have money either?"

"They are homeless, they probably don't have a job. And if they ask for money, I'm sure a lot of people aren't going to give them money."

"You said that if people don't have money, they should stay out as well and not come to church. What about babies? They have no money are you going to kick babies out too?"

"Now you're being ridiculous," replied Gary.

"I'm not the one being ridiculous, you're the one being a brainless idiot. You just sat here and told me that if people don't have money, they shouldn't be allowed to come to church without money. Now if anyone is lying, it's you," said Lucifer coldly.

"You know I didn't mean babies."

"Oh really? You said if 'no one didn't have money.' You even accused me of having people come to church with no money."

"I didn't mean babies," replied Gary.

"So you meant homeless people then?"

"No, I didn't mean them either. You're twisting my words," said Gary.

"I'm not twisting anything; don't backpedal now. Next time, you better be clear with your words. You better say exactly what you mean, or I'll keep calling you out on everything you say in this very present moment."

"I mean other people, not the homeless or babies," replied Gary.

"Well, answer me Gary. "What happens if someone was in the hospital or got fired or fell on tough times or their jobs closed down and they tried keeping up with all of their bills, but wound up not having any money left?" asked Lucifer.

"They should have saved money," replied Gary.

"You do realize how hard it is to save money right now? Gas prices are up, food prices are up, everything is expensive now," said Lucifer. "So if someone couldn't save up money, they still shouldn't be allowed in church?" asked Lucifer.

"That's right, if they haven't saved money, that's not my problem. That's their problem, because the bible talks about saving.

"In Proverbs 21:20, it says, 'There is treasure to be desired and oil in the dwelling of the wise; but a foolish man spendeth it up,'" said Gary.

Do you ever think like I said before, that something may have happened? When they have no money, even if they saved money, you don't know what could've happened. But that's my fault right?" asked Lucifer.

"You probably had something to do with it," replied Gary.

Lucifer sat back in the chair, fingers touching, resting up against his face. "Oh, and speaking about clothes, I will give you there are certain things you shouldn't wear to a church, like lingerie or pajamas, that's just disrespectful. Same goes for wearing just underwear, that shouldn't be allowed. Besides all that, some ministers wear what your human call jeans and a shirt, and some wear suits. Since when did you Christians make church a fashion show? Talking about what peopke look like and what shoes they wear? Since when was church about what people have on? Where does it say in the bible, in the new or old testament, that you can't wear jeans or 'dress down clothes' as you humans like to call them. Oh I'm sorry, God cares more about what you have than He does about your heart, right? Because there'll be a huge fashion show in heaven. There must be a new law God implemented, that the only way to get into heaven is by wearing specific types of clothes instead of being saved. As far as your definition of church, it's supposed to be God's house, where you come to love God, learn about God, and worship God. Then again, you can do all of that anywhere by loving Him, reading the bible and worshiping Him. Church is supposed to be a safe haven for people to come and partake of the service, that goes for both members and visitors. You have those places where you, what is it called? Oh yes, get exercise and where there are signs saying 'no judgment zone'. People come to church not to be judged and ridiculed by churchgoers, or the pastor. There's a certain thing called correction, and it's different from belittling. People that come to church don't go to hear what fools think about their clothes. They come to hear the word of God and how it applies to their life, to get prayed for, not to be stressed by concerns like 'Oh, if you don't pay this amount or this amount, you'll die, or you won't get blessed or prayed for.' They didn't come to church to play that game you humans call musical chairs, having ushers tell them after they just sat down, 'Oh no, you can't sit here, you need to sit up there,' or 'this seat is for so and so.' Coming to church is to hear about God, to get uplifted, and to be shown love. Not berated, low rated, talked about. The church is supposed to be a house of God, not some social circle with cliques. Not some gossiping ground, not some crucifixion ground. I'll get into that in a little while," said Lucifer. "I'm about to enjoy this," he added.

Gary was puzzled by Lucifer's remark. "What do you mean you're going to enjoy this?"

"Now my questions come into play. You wanted to know why I make people leave the church for good? That's your question to me? Why I, Lucifer, would waste my time making people leave the church."

"Well, ya, I want to know," replied Gary.

Lucifer started to laugh. "What makes you think I, Lucifer, would make someone leave the church? I don't have to. You stupid Christian do the work for me," Lucifer replied while laughing.

"How dare you say that, you don't know what you're talking about and you're lying now. You couldn't take being second fiddle to God. You failed miserably," Gary got up and put his finger in Lucifer's face. "You're not taking this seriously."

Lucifer replied in his demonic voice. His hands started to change, wings came out of his back and he started to change into his true form. He grabbed Gary by the finger. "I will break your finger if I have to," then he grabbed Gary by the neck, and slammed him into the wall. "You Christians think you know so much." He squeezed Gary's throat. "Understand one thing, you're a stupid mortal who can die with a snap of a finger or a snap of your neck. You're the one that wanted to talk, you're the one that wanted to get things off your chest. You're the one that asked God Himself to arrange this. Did I not say He admonished me to tell the truth, but now you're coming at me? What did I tell you about watching your mouth? I would love to snap your neck right now, not out of enjoyment, but to shut you up. Then again, I would be doing the world a favor getting rid of a fake Christian like you. What's the matter, nothing to say? Say something! Oh that's right, maybe you forgot that I told you how hard it would be for a mere human to talk to me in my true form." Lucifer squeezed his hand tighter around Gary's neck.

"Lucifer stop this now! What did I tell you?" said God.

Lucifer let Gary go and turned back into his mortal form. He straightened his clothes out.

"Gary, you wanted a meeting. I told him to tell the truth, and now he is. Don't provoke him, do you understand?" commanded God.

"Yes, I understand," replied Gary. "Sorry about that. I didn't mean to snap, but you made me mad, accusing Christians of doing something we never do."

"You do it all the time, you Christians and pastors. You do it so much you've made a habit out of it. You're the reason that people run away I don't have to do anything. You fake Christians want to make the church into a clique. You all have your groups and try to be holier than you are. I've seen people with more holiness in their little toenail than some of you have in your whole body."

CHAPTER 2

Lucifer went on, "So let me ask you this, how many Gods are there? How many Jesus' are there? How many Holy Ghosts are there? How many Lucifers are there?"

"There is only one God, one Jesus, One Holy Ghost, and only one Lucifer, which is you," replied Gary.

"Correct. One God, one Jesus, one Holy Ghost and one me. So tell me, what was that that came out of your mouth? About how I failed at attempting to be higher than God and couldn't stand being second fiddle? You mortals always say history repeats itself. Why do pastors think that they are God or above God?" asked Lucifer.

"What are you talking about?" replied Gary.

"Why is it that pastors say, 'Oh come into God's house,' when everything is fine, but when a member makes him mad by not giving money or even questioning him, the pastor then says, 'This is my church.' So which is it? God's house? Or is it the pastor's church? And before you say both, consider this: a person sends his butler to buy a house for him. The butler buys the house for his employer. The butler maintains the house and keeps it clean and makes sure that the people that enter into the house are entertained and treated well. Whose house is it?"

"Well, it's a different story," replied Gary.

"How is it different? God blesses the pastors to build a church. Everyone says the church is God's house. Pastors now want to think they're God. They say, 'Oh this is my church, if you don't like this and that, then get out.' They will also tell the whole congregation about, 'Oh this member left' and will start bad mouthing them, and the congregation follows their lead like blind sheep, 'Oh that's right pastor, you're telling the truth,' without even having a mind of their own. They should know for a fact that the member was a good person and did nothing wrong, but they will agree just because the pastor says so. Also, if a member disagrees with how the member leaving was handled, then they will get reprimanded and labeled a traitor or a turncoat and get talked about. You've done the same thing. To the one Mother that was at church. She did no wrong at all and your pastor low-rated her in front of the entire congregation. A few people didn't take part in that, but you and the others did. The thing is, he didn't call out her name, but you and the others knew who he was talking about. You saw her crying. She got up and left, and you all said the devil finally left. That Mother had more anointing in one strand of her hair then any of you put together. That was your doing, so don't blame that on me. You've all done it numerous times," said Lucifer. "That was God's child. You think I caused her to run off? See, this is where you all blame me for everything. That stops here. I was glad because she was sent there to help and try to pray for your big–ego, trash–talking, no–anointing-fool-of-a-pastor."

Gary remembered the time it happened.

Lucifer continued, "Let's get something straight. Pastors say all of this and feel no shame. Some do, and they repent. Others keep going and don't ask for forgiveness at all. Only thing some of them can do is ask for money, and then if they don't get money, they tell people in church and on the radio "Well, they better not call me, cause I'm not praying for them. They didn't give me an offering after all I've done for them.""

"But they shouldn't be prayed for. After a preacher prays for someone, the offerings they give go towards helping other people in ways like prophesying and healing," replied Gary.

"The gift is not theirs. They are renting it. The gifts are on loan from God," replied Lucifer coldly.

"Just like the woman you were talking about, how were we and the pastor supposed to know?" replied Gary.

"Look at **1 Thessalonians 5:**

> '11 *Wherefore comfort yourselves together, and edify one another, even as also ye do.*
>
> 12 *And we beseech you, brethren, to know them which labor among you, and are over you in the Lord, and admonish you;*
>
> 13 *And to esteem them very highly in love for their work's sake. And be at peace among yourselves.*
>
> 14 *Now we exhort you, brethren, warn them that are unruly, comfort the feeble-minded, support the weak, be patient toward all men.'*

"Your pastor is supposed to know who his sheep are. If all of you weren't doing all that talking, but were praying instead, you would've all known and kept your mouths shut. How were you to watch your pastor's back when you weren't praying for him and telling him listen? I think you may have been wrong about that one. You could have talked to him about it privately in his office. But that's the problem with pastors these days. They should have kept their thoughts about that woman to themselves. But, no, some pastors now want to tell everyone how they are feeling and bash someone in front of the church, and on radio, too. You Christians are no better, 'Oh I'm bishop this, I'm apostle that. Oh I'm evangelist this. Don't call me by my first name, you acknowledge me as Reverend. You better not call me John, it's bishop something-something to you.' You all care more about titles than anything. Titles don't give you power. God gives the power, not you. But, no, some of you Christians, all you want to do is seem so important and act like you have so much God in you, whenGod isn't even thinking about you because of how you act. Then you want to be like, 'Oh the devil is working in that person.' I don't even think about you or your church. God isn't in that church, it's just a building where you all play church. Remember what I said about pastors trying to act like God? Well, I want to know why some of you so-called Christians are trying to give me competition. We don't try to be like you. But you've done it for so long, you don't even realize it, but I'm going to point it out to you."

Lucifer went on to quote 1 Peter 5:8: "Be sober, be vigilant; because your adversary the devil, as a roaring lion, walketh about, seeking whom he may devour."

He went on to explain, "Pastors and you so-called Christians devour people's faith and happiness. Pastors say, 'Oh you're going to walk in church one way and leave out another way. That's one time some of these know-nothing pastors didn't lie, because some people come in feeling bad and leave feeling worse after having to listen to a whole bunch of foolishness.

'Oh you know, you need to put all your bills on hold and give unto God.' Sometimes, God didn't even ask this, they just say that. But then, that's the members' fault, because if they were praying like they were supposed to, God would let them know if He said for them to give or not.

"These pastors have a new lie now: 'Oh, if you give and it doesn't work, you come back and let us know, and we'll give you your money back,' knowing good and well if they asked for that money back, they'd feel insulted them or it would be as if you talked bad about their family. They know that if you asked, they wouldn't have the money to pay you back. And if you did come back, they'd talk behind your back and be like, 'Yeah, that was the devil the devil was using them.' All you stupid little sheep who can't think for themselves would be like, "That's right pastor, they are of the devil.' Telling that bold-faced lie in church, and I hate to say it, but you jackasses are more like my demons than my demons are, and that's an insult to my demons.

"Plus, these pastors, all they do is have their inner circle and talk about, 'Oh yes, God really moved for this person and that person. Oh, this person gave thousands of dollars. This person gave me their last and now they got their debts forgiven and have a new car,'" said Lucifer.

"Well, they probably did give their last," replied Gary.

"What about the people that don't have that much, huh? What about people that only have five dollars or twenty dollars and they give that, but nothing happens?"

"Maybe they did something wrong," Gary said.

"They didn't do anything wrong. The pastor is doing nothing but praying for their inner circle. Church is not supposed to be about cliques, and yeah, you can tell these pastors have favorites calling their name all the time and no one else's. The bible also says in **Isaiah 10:**

> 'Woe unto them that decree unrighteous decrees, and that write grievousness which they have prescribed; To turn aside the needy from judgment, and to take away the right from the poor of my people, that widows may be their prey, and that they may rob the fatherless!'

"You have pastors out here that have widows in their church but don't check on them to see if they are alright and don't check on them to see if they need anything. All they do is call when they need something from the widows, like money or if they are coming to service. They don't even check on the fatherless, or the ones that don't have parents. Tell me how?" asked Lucifer. "I want you to explain this to me, how a pastor has a member of the church that doesn't make a lot of money but writes them and says, 'Please pray. This is all the money I have right now. I'm giving this because I really need a breakthrough for my family and I need God to really move.' That person even says, 'I remember you telling a story how one person had nothing and gave pennies or a dollar and God moved.' The pastor doesn't even respond back. They can take the money but not respond back. How about when a member gives something from the heart and the pastor discards it like it's nothing at all and gives it away? Yet they call themselves spiritual fathers and mothers to the congregation but treat them like street urchins. How are they going to call themselves that and then act heartlessly? They don't treat their kids like that or their favorites. Church is not supposed to be who can pay their way to be the favorite of a pastor, and that whoever pays the most is the ones that get prayed for. You all talk about, 'Oh we want to be like Jesus.' Nowhere in the bible did Jesus treat anyone like you fake stuck up Christians and fake pastors treat people. Jesus never mistreated Mary Magdalene because of who she was, no he treated her with respect and kindness. He prayed for the blind man in **Mark 8:22-26:**

> 'And he cometh to Bethsaida; and they bring a blind man unto him, and besought him to touch him. And he took the blind man by the hand, and led him out of the town; and when he had spit on his eyes, and put his hands upon him, he asked him if he saw ought. And he looked up, and said, I see men as trees, walking. After that he put his hands again upon his eyes, and made him look up: and he was restored, and saw every man clearly. And he sent him away to his house, saying, neither go into the town, nor tell it to any in the town.'"

He continued, "Don't forget about John 5: After this there was a feast of the Jews; and Jesus went up to Jerusalem. Now there is at Jerusalem by the sheep market a pool, which is called in the Hebrew tongue Bethesda, having five porches. In these lay a great multitude of impotent folk, of blind, halt, withered, waiting for the moving of the water. For an angel went down at a certain season into the pool, and troubled the water: whosoever then first after the troubling of the water stepped in was made whole of whatsoever disease he had. And a certain man was there, which had an infirmity thirty and eight years. When Jesus saw him lie, and knew that he had been now a long time in that case, he saith unto him, Wilt thou be made whole? The impotent man answered him, Sir, I have no man, when the water is troubled, to put me into the pool: but while I am coming, another steppeth down before me. Jesus saith unto him, Rise, take up thy bed, and walk. And immediately the man was made whole, and took up his bed, and walked: and on the same day was the Sabbath.

Jesus, not once, asked these people for anything, and these preachers talk about not praying for anyone who don't give money. These preachers need to understand that even I, Lucifer, know that God is the one that does the blessing. These pastors want people to think it's about them, and it's not. These pastors are ruining it for the ones that are actually doing it right. The pastors and the church members talk about what this person had on or how much they gave, if they gave at all. Why haven't some members been showing up? You all have turned church into a joke. On occasions, I send people that my demons have possessed to churches, but not your church, because the only thing that will happen is that you and your pastor will get hurt and injured. You all have no anointing in your church. Plus, pastors are saying, 'Oh God told me this and God told me that.' God didn't even say 'hi' to them, much less give them a word. Pastors need to stop telling people that God gave them a word when He didn't. Because if they said that God said something and God didn't say it, that just makes people lose faith. Plus the way some of the people that have been treated by your church and other churches have made them choose other religions, commit suicide, or never take religion seriously. People think pastors are a joke. People think God is a joke. People have turned science into a religion. Pastors will have their ministers to call and make small talk just to be like, 'Oh well, you heard the word that pastor, or apostle, or bishop or prophet had for you? And you know we need help.'

A person will give five dollars and that will be their last. But before the person can catch another breath, that so-called minister will be like, 'Oh no problem. You know, if you feel like giving more, you can.' Or, 'Would you like to pledge a thousand dollars, or whatever God lays on your heart? You can make monthly payments towards it.' Yet I'm the one who ends up blamed for this.

"You know what, I appreciate it, because then people who really have a love for God wind up feeling scammed, and turn away from God and go somewhere else to find what they couldn't find at that certain church or from that certain pastor.

"Members of that church will call during the day late at night or even when people are at work. They have no consideration. Pastors are sleeping with congregation members, cheating on their spouses. The media gets a hold of that and makes it all look bad for the church, but they don't care at all.

"You fake Christians are sending people to me in droves. I'm glad you send them to me, because it's like you're working for me. People come to me when you Christians are playing church and saying God said this and that when He never did. Instead of going and seeking true prophets, they get had by con men, or some may have had a legit calling, but sold their soul to me in the end. People now go to psychics, witches, and witch doctors and practice voodoo. Why? Because they went to the church and didn't get treated with respect or were told because they didn't have a lot of money or a certain amount, they would not get prayed for. Or they would come to church and church wouldn't start until an hour later. Or they had preachers that would talk about politics. Or they heard people get bashed and talked about. So they come to me for what you Christians couldn't give them. God sends people to some churches to pray for the pastor and the church. Or they come seeking help, and God gives that minister a chance to do what's right and they don't. You so-called loving congregations treat people like lepers. You think you are too good for them because you hang out with the pastor.

"God gives people chances and you all squander those chances and don't do what's right. Fake Christians will not be there to uplift anybody.

The only thing you fake Christians do is brutalize, beat down, mock, make fun of, insult and tear down people. There is something called chastisement and correction that you don't even do. You're supposed to chastise and correct with love and build people back up. But not you all, you just cast your judgments upon people for what they wear and what they don't have. You fake Christians would have never been able to be with Jesus because you all would have been the first to crucify Him. You all would have been part of the Sanhedrin. You would have never have lasted even a second, back in the days of Moses, Abraham, David, and Jesus. No, you all would have gotten mad at what he had to say and would have been called out by the disciples.

"Let me ask you a question, Gary. Back in the day, in the fifties, sixties, seventies, eighties, nineties, do you think I had more freedom then or more freedom now?"

"I would say back then," replied Gary.

Lucifer laughed, "You would be wrong. Because back then, there used to be more mothers praying in church, lifting up a stronghold against me. I could barely do anything. People were praying more and were more about God then they are now. The old mothers died out, and I was celebrating because of that. If you look around right now and see everything that is going on in this world, you can tell I have more freedom and people aren't praying as much. Look around at what's being signed into bills and look at what's going on in the world. I talk to your politicians all over the world. I convince them to make the decisions they make. So I have almost full reign. I say 'almost' because God is only letting me get away with so much. Another way I get more freedom is by people trying to act like God. You have scientists trying to clone other animals, and how do you know they haven't tried it on people yet? If you say because it's not on the news, well, they don't tell everyone everything. You will never find out about new weapons or diseases that are being created. You won't ever be told that humans are being experimented on for some depraved scientific research. You will never find out about that. I If it ever leaks out, the people that leaked it will die and the governments will make all of that disappear. See, if everyone was really and sincerely praying, half the things that are going on never ever would have made it through.

"You all must have forgotten that God brought about the plagues in Egypt. He wanted His people to be let go. So if he did that then and swallowed up the people that were worshiping the golden calf while Moses was up on the mountain getting the ten commandments… God is a jealous god, and the fact that people are worshiping everything, different gods, false gods, science… The fact that you fake Christians are messing up God's children, that can only lead to disaster. You think there is deliverance for these so-called pastors who have backslidden and have been given opportunity after opportunity to get it right with God and for all you people in the congregation that follow everything the pastor says without thinking for yourself and know the pastor is in the wrong? You think there will be mercy for how he tears down people's faith and spirit as they go home crying because they think that they did something wrong or that God doesn't love them? You fake Christian have blood on your hands, and because of the acts you all have committed, you're drowning in blood.

"I'm telling you the utmost truth right now, and that is Judgment is coming and it's going to fall and it's going to fall hard and fast and you all will be crying, wondering why all of this is happening. You have let worldly, ungodly, demonic things into the churches. You have bought things into churches that should be left home or out in the world. You bring it to church and incorporate it into services. That's why people of the world don't respect you. If you all were doing what was right and what was required, people would be coming to church and more souls would be saved. Respect has been lost. That's why you see on these things called social media people insulting and cursing out pastors and trying to fight pastors. None of this went on in the sixties and seventies or anytime in the nineties. People were too scared that God would strike them down. There was more reverence. There is none of that anymore. People need to understand that it's not their place. And this goes for all people, not just the fake Christians. But it's not your job to expose anyone, it's God's job, and I help with exposing. I have nothing to fear from you or from your church and these fake people. Sometimes, I'll send a possessed person into one of those services with a fake pastor, and when they can't cast the demon out, then they get hurt and are made to look stupid. I fear the ones who are really dedicated and serve God, they have power.

CHAPTER 3

The bible also says in Ezekiel 34:1-6—And the word of the Lord came unto me, saying, Son of man, prophesy against the shepherds of Israel, prophesy, and say unto them, thus saith the Lord God unto the shepherds; Woe be to the shepherds of Israel that do feed themselves! Should not the shepherds feed the flocks? Ye eat the fat, and ye clothe you with the wool, ye kill them that are fed: but ye feed not the flock. The diseased have ye not strengthened, neither have ye healed that which was sick, neither have ye bound up that which was broken, neither have ye brought again that which was driven away, neither have ye sought that which was lost; but with force and with cruelty have ye ruled them. And they were scattered, because there is no shepherd: and they became meat to all the beasts of the field, when they were scattered. My sheep wandered through all the mountains, and upon every high hill: yea, my flock was scattered upon all the face of the earth, and none did search or seek after them.

"Some of these pastors care only for themselves and nothing about their congregation. When the pastors drive away God-filled people and make them leave the church, they just leave them out there and don't go out there to find them, bring them back or even apologize to them. A pastor is supposed to be caring and uplifting and give correction when needed. A pastor is assigned to his flock. To lead and guide them and teach them the ways of God.

"Why do you bring the world into the church with singing and dancing?" asked Lucifer.

"Because we try to help bring people into the church," replied Gary.

"Since when does God need your help? God wouldn't be God if he needed your help. Some of you fake Christians want to walk around with a title and then want to flirt with other people whilst you're married. You don't respect anybody. You tell people you're a deacon or a pastor or a minister, and don't know how to treat anyone.

"When people go around telling others that they have a title in church and then act like they are better than others and do whatever they like, they curse, they start fights, they cheat, they are whoremongers, they belittle people who are not even in the church. Pastors that hear from God for elevating a member to a calling like bishop, evangelist, prophet, or apostle and God gives them the people he wants elevated, but then they disobey God and elevate people that God didn't call because they're scared of leaving one of their favorites out.

Another thing with you humans, you all want to be in full control of your lives and everything and leave God out of it. Some of you say, 'Oh I'm giving it to God,' but some of you don't because you all get mad when God doesn't do what you want the very second you ask him for something. You do know He knows more than any of you. He's God and He knows when to and when not to give you something. You all wouldn't know what to do if God gave you what you were asking for. All you would do is make a mess out of it. I come in and interfere and make you think that God has no intention of helping you, but you all are so quick to give up. I'll take credit for some of the cases, but some of it is just a test to see if you can handle what you're asking God for. Plus, why don't any of you pray for your enemies to get saved? No, all you all want is murder, death, and plagues to fall upon them. And yes, some of them I do use. But some I don't. You ever think maybe you should pray for them to get saved and for God to change their hearts instead of wishing and praying for death upon them and their families? You fake Christians talk good, but can you back it up? Remember what I said about pastors always wanting money. Well, you should also take into account that you should give something if they have been praying for you all the time, and come and visit you in the hospital and your family members. It's an act of decency for the pastors that do take time out to call and make sure you're okay or even perform weddings and do funerals. You should have it in your heart to give them something because after all, you should say 'thank you' when someone does something nice for you. Yes you don't have to, but you also have to think about the pastors who are preaching and praying and who never take a break and run themselves down.

"You Christians need to take that into consideration. You all need to stop worshiping pastors and preachers as God. Yes, you should hold them to a higher standard, but they are not God, no matter how some of the fake pastors want to act. Preachers and pastors are human. They bleed, they get tired and they make mistakes. That's why you need to pray before you decide to go to a church.

"Do you have any more questions?" asked Lucifer.

"No, I'm just in shock because I never expected this to happen."

"You asked to have this talk with me and I was commanded to tell the truth.

Our time here has come to an end. I suggest you keep in mind what was talked about because like I said, Judgment is coming and it's a lot closer than you think. It's just around the corner and these Christians and fake Christians and these pastors and preachers who are not treating God's children right will have a heavy price to pay."

With that, Lucifer disappeared and Gary fell asleep. When Gary woke up, he got up and looked around and looked throughout his house and saw no sign of Lucifer, or even any trace of him even being there. It must've been a dream.

It was Sunday and Gary went to a service. He saw his pastor go off and talk about how people need to pay in that church and called everyone out by name that hadn't paid and embarrassed them. Just as Gary was about to agree, he looked up and saw Lucifer in his human form. Lucifer leaned up against the podium with his legs crossed and waved and smiled at Gary.

Gary started to remember the whole night when he asked God to speak to Lucifer and everything that was said. Gary felt convicted and left the church that day and never came back. He saw the old members of that church and they talked about him like a dog and said he was no good and a traitor.

Gary walked away. "God I realize now everything I did was wrong. The way I treated people, the way the church treats your people. Please forgive me of all my wrongdoing and everything I've done against you and your people. Please forgive me, make me pure and cleanse me, make me whole. Come into my life and save me this day. I'm truly sorry for everything I did, forgive me of all things I've done and may very well do, in Jesus' name. Amen."

With those words, Gary's life was changed. He never again mistreated God's people. He went and told his story. Some people didn't believe him or very few did believe him. He saw on the news where a sinkhole formed and swallowed all the old members of the church including the pastor.

"You escaped me, but now that you changed your life around, I will be coming for you more and more." Gary jumped and turned around.

It was Lucifer who then disappeared.

I want to thank My mom and
My dad for always believing in me.

I would like to thank my grandma and my Uncle James
and Uncle Chip for looking down on me from heaven and
watching out for me.

I would like to thank Brother Charles Hunter
for his prayers for my books.

I would like to thank
Pastor Edna Woodward for her prayers.

I would like to thank Mary Thompson
for all her prayers and support.

I would also like to thank
Effie Langley for all of her prayers.

www.ingramcontent.com/pod-product-compliance
Lightning Source LLC
LaVergne TN
LVHW020447080526
838202LV00055B/5374